CU01212716

Pavor Nocturnus

Scott M. Stockton

This is a work of fiction. Names, characters, businesses, places, events, and incidents are either the product of the author's imagination or used in a fictitious manner. Any resemblance to actual persons, living or dead, is purely coincidental.

Copyright 2017 by Scott M. Stockton
All Rights Reserved

"The oldest and strongest emotion of mankind is fear, and the oldest and strongest kind of fear is fear of the unknown."

— H.P. Lovecraft

Introduction

My name is Kathleen Bell.   What I'm about to tell you is nothing of the average.   You may think, *this is just another horror story told by a writer with a big imagination*, but I'm not here to tell you what is real and what isn't.   That is for you to decide.   Ever since I was a young girl, I've suffered from frequent nightmares.   Granted, as I grew older they've seemed to dissipate, but they still return to this day.   These were not your regular nightmares.   I was once told they could've been "night terrors" which are common among young children.   These dreams would haunt me on a nightly basis, waking me to the point of screaming out through sleep.   I would see things you couldn't even imagine…and still haven't forgotten.   By my early teenage years, I was prescribed a medication to help me sleep.   I would go to weekly therapy sessions to try and relieve my thoughts and this problem.   It seemed to stop for a while…but would always come back.   I felt possessed.   As though something had this hold on me, and was not letting go.   Making me see things, and scaring me to point I thought I might die.   I know…this seems overdramatic, but if you saw what I've seen…you'd feel the same.   A few doctors even suggested this problem was caused by a trauma I went through when I was a girl.   That would be a highly possible explanation...if that were actually the case.   The thing is...there is no record of something like that happening to me, so it was ruled out.

I noticed, that as I grew older, the dreams would slowly quiet themselves, and only bother me a couple of times a week, soon less than that. My parents figured they would soon disappear forever, and I'd be just like everyone else.   I started to believe that, and felt better about it.   I started babysitting around seventeen, as a side job while still in school.   Many didn't know about my nightmare problem outside the family, and I was known as a trustworthy person, so this was good for me.   However, this luck changed after one night of watching over the Stafford's kids.   Ed and Mary Stafford knew me for years, since just living four blocks down from me.   They had two kids named Matthew and Heather.   Matty being the elder of the two, at twelve years old, while Heather merely just turned ten on her birthday three days before this.   Mary asked me to come over the night before Halloween, and since I wasn't busy much that night, I accepted.   She and Ed wanted to go out for a few hours to have some time together before the holiday.   What happened that night...is something I'll never forget.

Chapter 1

October 30th, 7:15pm

Oil City, Pennsylvania

While sitting on her bed with a book in hands, Kathleen lightly began to twirl her fingers softly in her long dark brown hair.   Usually kept straight, it often dangled over the sides of her face whenever she sat like this.   Her large and thick history book lay over her lap for a better balance, letting her homework paper sit on the side page. She'd been wanting to finish all of her assignments before Halloween, since making previous plans to go out with friends that night, and didn't want to have it in the way of her fun time.   Her friends often called her Kathy, as did everyone else.   She didn't mind being called Kathleen, but her nickname was shorter to say.

Removing her circular shaped silver glasses, Kathy gently rubbed her brown eyes from the tired feeling of staring down at the book for the past hour. The night before had been a battle of sleep, as her nightmares like to taunt her mind now and then. She was soon to be an adult, as her eighteenth birthday dawned near in the next month. She didn't feel too old to go out for Trick or Treating, and dress up in a costume, and she hoped she'd have enough sleep to go out with her friends. Since the nightmares had recurred the night before, it usually meant they would again the next night, or the next sleep. They seemed to come in waves, even though they dwindled down some from when she was younger.

After hearing a knock on her bedroom door, Kathy looked up from her bed and called out in a light voice.
"It's open" she said. With a turn of the brass knob, a head full of long blond curly hair peaked around the doorframe, as a smile came following. Kathy returned a tired smile of her own at the sight of her friend. "Hi Lonna."
"What'cha doin' up here all by yourself?" the girl asked, stepping inside the room. She flopped herself down upon the bed with her tiny white purse falling to the floor lazily.
"Just finishing up my slave work" Kathy said in mild humor, poking the pages of her history book. Lonna laughed for a moment at her friend's remark, and laid herself down over the end of the bed; her legs draping off the side as she stared at the ceiling.
"Oh hermit Kathy...you need to get out and

away from this dismal room once in a while.   You spend too much time in here sometimes"   Lonna teased.   Kathy shot a glare at the blonde girl lying ahead of her and closed the study book.

"We're going out tomorrow night, and my room is not dismal.   Nor am I a hermit"   she countered.   "I just wanted this done before we go out for candy."

Lonna turned her head with placid face, staring back at her friend.   Reaching over with her finger, and poking the spine of the book as she spoke.

"You know Zach will be coming with us too, right?   He's been wanting to see you again."

Kathy pulled her book back against her, fishing through the pages in a somewhat annoyed manner at the mention of the boy's name.   Giving a sigh, she stabbed the tip of her pencil in the center of the paper's top margin.

"Lonna, I told you before…Zach and I are over.   We just…don't get along."

After a flustered look, Lonna leaned herself up on her side as she lounged there indefinitely.

"Now is that *really* how you feel about him, or are you just running away again?"   she asked her.   "You know that everyone's entitled to *one* mistake."

Looking up from the book, Kathy's still glare of irritation could be felt in Lonna's eyes.

"I'm not coming if he's there"   she said shortly.   She looked off to her side as the book fell on the bed blanket without care.   She closed her eyes gently and spoke again.   "Sometimes one mistake is all it takes."

   Lonna stared at her friend for a long minute of silence.   As Kathy's head was turned away, she could see a small tear in her right eye beginning to form.   Zach had indeed hurt Kathy's feelings pretty badly when he cheated, but she didn't want to see her friend constantly down and depressed. The previous day, the boy had come to Lonna for assurance that she'd talk with Kathy for him and see if the girl would give him another chance…because he apparently couldn't confront her, himself.   To no avail, his plan was not working, and Lonna knew it should be *him* talking with Kathy instead of *her*.

   "Alright…if that's how you feel about it, then he doesn't have to come with us.   I won't push it any further.   I'm sorry"   she said.   Kathy looked back again and seemed to breathe a calmer sigh before slowly holding her arms around her friend for comfort.   Lonna patted her friend's back lightly, whispering in reassurance.   "You know I'm here for you too…you'll get through this….I promise."

   Kathy smiled to herself when hearing her friend's words, and leaned back again, closing her book.   A soft knocking at the door jogged the girls' attention as Kathy's mother stepped inside the room, holding a phone in her hand.

   "Kathy dear, Mrs. Stafford is asking if you'll baby-sit tonight.   Is that alright with you?   I know you have some work to finish, so I can tell her that you're busy" she asked her.   Quiet for a moment, Kathy then nodded to her mother and smiled.

"It's alright, tell her I'll be right over.   I'll just finish this after the kids go to bed tonight" she said.   The woman left the room with the phone, and Kathy reached over to her computer desk for her car keys.   She then grabbed a blue carry-on bag to put her homework books into it.

"Have fun watching little demons tonight…maybe I should go with you"   Lonna teased.   She grinned at her friend, whom smiling back, poked her friend in the forehead before walking toward the door.

"You and I both know, if you come with me, you'll just be in it for the food"   she said, teasing back.   It was no secret that Lonna loved to eat, and more specifically, loved to eat other people's food.   She was a poor house guest when it came to this habit.   Kathy often wondered how her waistline could stay so thin.   "And besides, you're going out to dinner with your grandma tonight. It's her birthday, right?"

Lonna stood up quickly from the bed, and shut the door behind her as she and Kathy walked down the staircase.

"Yeah, she turned sixty today, so my mom and I are taking her to Red Lobster"   Lonna clarified.   "She has this big thing for seafood, as you know."

After saying their goodbyes, Lonna drove off in her car as Kathy walked out to her own in the driveway.   Unlocking the door of her 1990 Pontiac LeMans coupe, red in color, the girl's mother followed her outside.

"Will you be back late again?"   she asked her, standing by the door.   Kathy rolled down the window and started the engine.

"Probably.   They always stay out 'till like, midnight or one in the morning"   she responded. Noticing her daughter had blinked her eyes a total of six times now, her mother became cautious.

"Be careful driving tonight.   You need to take those sleeping pills.   They'll help"   she suggested.   Without speaking, Kathy held up the bottle of pills from her purse for her mother to see, and then drove down the driveway to the street.

Even though she knew her family and friends were only concerned about her, and after years of having a nightmare problem, Kathy still felt they didn't trust her enough to do things for herself.   Stopping at the red-light, she looked down at the pill bottle on the passenger seat beside her, lying next to her purse.   Originally meant to help her sleep, she was told the medicine would also work to calm her nerves if needed, and relax her.   Reaching over for it, she popped one of the tiny pinkish capsules down her throat with a swallow of Brisk iced tea.   Tossing the bottle back to her purse, she clutched the steering wheel and spoke allowed to herself in the car lightly.

"There…I took the damn thing" she sighed. "I doubt it'll work anyway."

Her gaze on the road ahead of her was soon interrupted by another car's horn behind her. Looking up at the stoplight, she realized she'd been sitting at a green-light, and others were waiting behind her to go. Stepping on the gas, she followed the next two blocks down to the Stafford's place, a mid-sized Tudor styled home complete with an elegant bay window toward the front, where the living room was.

Parking her little Pontiac along the side out front of the house, Kathy was soon greeted by Mrs. Stafford, herself. The woman came walking down the front pathway as Kathy locked her car and showed a smile. Her carry-on bag was draped on her shoulder as she stepped up the front steps.

"I'm so glad you could make it tonight, and just in time too" the woman said. "How've you been, dear?" She and the girl came into the living room, seeing Matthew and Heather sitting on the couch, watching TV.

"I'm doing okay" Kathy replied, even though it'd been a white lie. "Are you and Mr. Stafford planning an evening?" she asked her.

The woman nodded to the girl, looking down at her watch and feeling slightly rushed. Walking toward the back of the home, through the dining room, was the kitchen. The entire right side of the house itself was the living room after first entering, followed by the dining and kitchen area going toward the backend.   Featured in the kitchen's nook, was yet another large bay window that allowed views of the back lawn, stretching up into a small inclining hill at the base of the forest nearby.   The rear driveway was just before the detached garage near the rear entrance of the home.   While looking through the large windows, one could see directly through the home with a straight shot glance, being able to look from the front yard to the back easily.   Or vice versa, depending on your position.   The left side consisted of the home's parlor, library, and study room, as Mr. Stafford had been a college professor for most of his years.   Kathy has always liked coming here, even though the Stafford's were always away for long hours.   She could tour the large house while they were gone, and the kids were sleeping.

"Help yourself to anything in the fridge if you get hungry, you know I don't mind.   Ed and I will most likely be gone until 1am, but I expect the kids to be in bed by 9:30"   Mary explained.   The woman turned her head and soon could see the tiredness in the eyes of the girl standing in front of her with a quiet smile.   "You look rather tired...are you sure you want to baby-sit tonight? I could find someone else."

Kathy spoke up, and lifted her bag off her shoulder that held her books and cell phone inside.

"No, it's alright.   I have some homework to

finish, and my night is free.   You go have a good time with your husband, we'll be okay here"   she assured.   Mary smiled again, and nodded before grabbing her coat to leave out the back door to Mr. Stafford waiting in a white Cadillac in the driveway.

"Alright, have a nice night, Kathy.   We'll try and get back before midnight.   I trust you, so I'm glad you could come at the last minute"   the woman said, giving a wave goodbye and entering the luxury car.   Kathy waved in return as the Stafford's drove off, and walked back into the living room.

Matthew and Heather were busy watching cartoons when Kathy came back, and after placing her bag on the coffee table, the younger girl leaned over curiously peeking into it.

"Whatcha got there?"   she asked her. Kathy sat down on the chair near them, and leaned back to relax.

"Just some homework.   I brought it 'cause I have to finish it before tomorrow comes.   It's almost Halloween after all"   she said with a wink and a smile.   Heather grinned widely at the mention of the holiday, and stood up with her hands on her hips.

"I'm going to be a witch for Halloween!" she declared with excitement.   "My mom even got *green* make-up to put all over my face!"   Her wide grin was placed over her lips entirely after making her proud statement, and then poked Kathy's shoulder. "What are *you* gonna be?" she asked her.

"I haven't decided yet. Maybe a vampire" Kathy replied, matching the younger girl's grin. She looked over at Matthew sitting on the far end of the couch with a look of boredom on his face. His longish brown hair draping near his eyes was messy and uncombed. He'd grown a bit since the last time she'd seen him, probably hitting a growth spurt. "What about *you*, Matty? Any thought on what you'll be for Halloween?"

The boy was silent, and shrugged his shoulders lightly as he began to blush, knowing the older girl was looking over at him. Matthew Stafford had a small crush on Kathy for a while now, and was feeling embarrassed about having her as his babysitter. His younger sister jumped at the question with a loud voice once again.

"He's gonna be a devil!" she announced with pride. "I think it fits him…he's always so *mean* to me, Kathy!" Heather admitted. Matthew soon tossed a throw pillow at Heather's head as it hit and bounced off quickly. The girl gave a short scream, and then looked at Kathy for a rescue. "*See* what I mean?! He's *always* like that…and not to mention he *liiiikes* you too…"

"Shut up jerk-face!" Matthew confronted, smacking yet another pillow onto Heather's head. The girl ran into Kathy's arms with a sinister giggle as Matthew got up from the couch, and ran into the next room.

"Aww…Matty…it's okay…I don't mind.

You can stay in here with us" Kathy called to him. With no reply from the boy, Kathy soon gave up and decided he'd come back when he was ready to. Heather, having felt satisfied with her taunt, sat herself back on the couch again to watch more cartoons, letting her blonde pigtails dangle in her hair; one of them knocked loose from Matthew's pillow attack. Kathy smiled at the thought of them, remembering how she and Lonna used to be like that when they were younger. Kathy may not have had siblings, but Lonna had two younger brothers, each just one year apart from each other. She laughed at the memory of when they would tease her brothers from time to time, during sleepovers with a few of Lonna's other friends.

After looking at the grandfather clock standing in the living room nearby, and seeing it was just nearing 8pm now, Kathy took out her homework books and decided she better finish it before the night was over.

Chapter 2

October 30, 8:45pm

After little over half an hour, Kathy finally finished what she planned to do. Closing the covers of her history book, she seen how by this time, Heather had fallen asleep soundly on the couch while the TV went ongoing in the background. It was dark now, and the two lamps in the living room glowed softly through the room, as she stared straight ahead of her. The window of the kitchen's nook held a slightly haunting effect as it reflected the lamps in darkness. She could just barely see the back lawn, and the hill as it sloped upward into the thickened black forest of pines and oak trees. There were small curtains on the window, just two decorative ones on either side near the top, to accent the kitchen's yellow and white coloring. They were checkered, and Kathy personally thought the design was ugly in choice, but this was not her home, so she shrugged it off. Wind had picked up a bit, letting her know a distant storm could be approaching or passing over, but it wasn't strong.   Now and then she could hear the branches of the trees rustling about outside the house, but there was no rain or thunder and lightning.

She grabbed the remote for the television and shut it off, leaving the remaining noise of the room left to the tall grandfather clock standing nearby.   Swaying its large brass pendulum, an aged and deep ticking sound flowed from it as she looked over at it curiously.   She wondered how old it had been; probably thirty years or more, due to its old-fashioned design, but she could never be sure.   She held no knowledge of clocks really, it was just something to think about as she sat there. It was boring in the large home, sitting on the sofa and looking around at objects from another family's life.

A sudden short 'ding' caught Kathy's attention from her mind, as she noticed her cell phone gave an alert.   She picked it up, and saw a text from Lonna asking if she was bored or having fun.   She smiled at the phone, the white screen lighting up her face as she spoke to it, as if Lonna could hear her.

"You're like a psychic sometimes, Lonna" she quietly said allowed.   Looking over at Heather, she saw the girl slightly move in her sleep from the sound of Kathy's voice, but hadn't woken. Her tiny arm, loosely dangled over the edge of the couch as she began to drool on the throw pillow. This made Kathy chuckle softly, thinking the girl was cute while sleeping. She texted back a 'just peachy' message to Lonna, and closed her phone again. Remembering Matthew previously left the room, she wondered why he didn't come back yet.

Leaving the living room and walking through the parlor area, Kathy took in a mental image map of the home as she strolled. The entirety of the house was dark, except the living room, so she lit a few lamps along the way, while softly calling out Matthew's name. She knew he wasn't upstairs in his room, for the living room held the location of the staircase. She would've seen him walk by her.

There was a small hallway that went along the center of the home, seeming to connect both sections of the lower portion of the house. From in this hall, Kathy could see the entrances to all the rooms on the first floor, except the kitchen area. The only doorway to the kitchen was in the dining room, aside from the rear outside entrance. The house was larger inside than what it seemed from the exterior, and most houses were like that. The parlor was the first room to be seen when walking through the front main entrance. From there everything branched off, including the hall.

Deciding not to bother with the hall's light, as she could see a glow of lighting coming from underneath the closed door of the library room, Kathy walked toward it, knowing the boy must be inside. With a slow turn of the knob, she looked in, finding Matthew staring down at a book as he sat in a lounge chair. He looked up at her when she entered, and closed the book in his hands.

"Hey Matty, how long you been here?" she asked him, striking conversation. The boy shrugged, beginning to blush again as he pinched the tip of the book's cover on the corner edge.

"I dunno...a while I guess" he said shyly. Kathy smiled, walking over to the boy and knelt down beside him in the chair. He slowly turned his head a bit, trying not to look at her. "*What?*..." he asked.

"Matty, listen,...I know you have a little crush on me...and its okay. I'm cool with it. I just want you to know that you don't have to be shy around me. I won't bite ya" she said to him. Giving a sigh, Matthew looked at the girl and blinked his eyes a few times before speaking normally.

"I'm just....embarrassed I guess. You're the first girl I ever liked...and I'm sure a lot of guys like you...and you probably got a boyfriend, so just forget it" he said clearly. Kathy laughed lightly, shaking her head a bit and stood up. Matthew noticed this, and was slightly offended. "What's so funny? I meant what I said..." he voiced in aggravation.

"Nothing, really Matty. And I don't have a boyfriend. But you need to know, that I'm your babysitter. I'm here to watch you while your mom and dad are gone, and that's all" she told him. Lifting an eyebrow, Matthew got up from the chair and tossed the book on the table next to him.

"I'm old enough to take care of myself....you don't need to *watch* me" he boldly said to her. "And...besides...its kinda weird having a girl I like be my babysitter."

Standing next to him, Kathy sighed and then smiled again to calm herself, and the boy with her.

"Then don't think of it that way. Just think of us as friends hanging out, and I'm here to watch your sister instead. Which...is basically true anyway. You don't cause trouble for me, unlike she does" Kathy explained. Matthew blinked again, reassured in what the girl told him, and showed a slight smile.

"Okay, cool. Just friends hanging out then. No little kid babysitter stuff for me."

Kathy reached over and shook his hand, giving a wink to him in return and walked toward the door of the room.

"It's a deal" she said. Before either of them could leave the room, a quick tap sound hit the window of the library from outside, almost like a short blare from a rock hitting the glass, although there was no mark or crack. The sound was loud enough to startle both Kathy and Matthew as they looked over at the window together.

"What was that?" she asked him, her eyes slightly wide for a moment. Matthew shrugged again, having his head turned and not showing the fact his eyes were wide as hers.

"I...dunno...it happened earlier too. I

heard it before, but it only happened once" he said.

Staring at the window, both could see the glass was unharmed, but couldn't tell if someone or something was standing outside, due to the pitch darkness from the night. Kathy heard a distant moan from the wind again, and figured it was probably just a small branch that hit the window.

"I...guess it was the wind" she said to him, and turned to leave the room back to the living room.

"Y-Yeah...like they always say" Matthew replied. He slowly closed the door behind him, leaving the light to library room on, not bothering to go back in and turn it off again.

It was now just after 9pm, as what Kathy confirmed after seeing the grandfather clock again, and hearing its chime when she and Matthew were walking back. Heather woke from the sound of their footsteps and sat up on the couch with her long blonde hair falling out of its pigtails. Matthew found a comfortable spot on the sofa loveseat near the large window in the room, where Kathy had been sitting, and Heather smiled up at the girl.

"I had a dream about you. You made me a bunch of cookies...but didn't share...and only gave them to Matty" she told her, making a frown. Kathy chuckled again, and knelt down beside the girl, giving her a small hug.

"You know if I ever made cookies, I'd give them all to you, Heather" she said with a grin. Heather smirked, and stuck her tongue out at her brother across the room, who in return, rolled his eyes with a "whatever" in sarcastic tone.

Kathy walked over to the loveseat, sitting down beside Matty as she opened her phone again, to view another text message from Lonna. Matthew blushed further, and quickly spoke.

"Do you…want me to get up? You look kinda tired…I can get up! I'll uh…let you have the loveseat."

Kathy shrugged a bit, and went back to texting on her phone as Matty stood up to go sit on the couch with his sister.

"Doesn't matter to me. I'm fine really" she said to him. Even though she indeed felt tired, Kathy chose to lay back on the loveseat with her legs propped over the side arm to relax, and text on her phone. "In a half an hour you both have to go to bed for me, okay?" she said to them, without looking away from the phone's screen. Heather whined slightly, but after a nudge from her older brother, she soon stopped, poking at his arm for her own amusement. Laying down on her side, and placing her cell phone on the coffee table, Kathy pressed her cheek softly on the pillow of the loveseat, staring over at the television which Matthew turned on again. He lowered the volume to a dull sound, and Heather laid down again as well, feeling bored with herself. The voices of the people in the electronic black box seemed to merge together as Kathy stared at them. Her eyes were falling heavy, slowly coming together and her body felt very lazed.   The pill she took earlier in her car was taking effect, and she wondered if she would stay awake.   Looking at the kids near her in the room, she knew she must stay awake.   Stay awake…and stay awake…watch over them…and keep them safe…until their mother came home.   Her eyes falling completely closed, she kept saying it in her mind, to stay awake, and stay awake…watch over them…and keep them safe.   It was like a chant now.   Playing over in her mind on a rolling walkway, a record, turning faster in her mind like a turntable.   Her legs running on the scroll as she ran toward Matthew and Heather, both of them drifting further away in the room as it stretched ongoing into a blur of colors and objects mashing together as one.   Was she dreaming?   No…she was awake, she must stay awake…and watch over them…keep them safe.

It was nothing short of a violent shaking as Kathy opened her eyes again to focus.   Standing over her was Heather, calling to her with streaming tears down her cheeks as she tried to wake Kathy up again.   Her words were too fast, and she couldn't understand what the girl was saying.   Only something about a shadow at the window, and Matthew had seen it.   Something about teeth and blood on the glass with scratching sounds.

Kathy sat up to find Heather and Matthew still watching TV as she sat there. Her heart was pounding wildly in her chest, trying to catch up with her breaths as she stared ahead at the children. Matthew turned around and could see her breathing hard, but for what reason, he didn't know. He stood up quickly, running over and knelt beside on the floor.

"Kathy…what's wrong? You okay?" he asked her. Heather came over too, tugging gently on the girl's arm with a worried look.

"Did you have a bad dream, Kathy?" she questioned. Kathy felt as though she was smothered, and stood up from the loveseat in fast motion, almost knocking young Heather to the floor. Matthew stared up at her with eyes full of uncertainty and grabbed his sister's arm to pull her away.

"What the hell Kathy!" he said strongly. "You almost knocked her over…what's wrong with you?"

Standing there beside them, Kathy placed her hands over her eyes, rubbing them slowly as she moved her fingers up her forehead, trying to collect herself again. Her long dark brown hair fell over her face, and she pushed it back slowly.

"I…was just having a nightmare…that's all. Sorry guys…didn't mean to scare you" she said to them. Heather broke free from her brother's grasp and ran to hug Kathy around the waist.

"It's okay. What was your dream about?"

she asked with curious eyes.   Kathy was reluctant to say, and simply began to shake her head in a 'no' response, looking up at the grandfather clock at the same time.   She realized it was almost 10:00pm and both Matthew and Heather should've been in bed a half hour ago.   She knew for sure now, that she had fallen asleep for almost an hour.

"You both should be in bed.   I'm sorry I fell asleep, so don't tell your mom on me, okay?   You both got to stay up a little longer than normal, so let's just keep that between us"   she told them. The chimes for the clock sounded at the approach of the hour, and Kathy looked down at her cell phone, seeing she'd missed three texts from Lonna.   Her friend had gone back home by now, and was wondering how her night was going with the kids.   Quickly texting back, she explained how she fell asleep, and was now sending them to bed so she could relax again.   Meanwhile, Lonna stared at her cell phone's screen with a baffled look, wondering why her friend fell asleep in the first place while babysitting.   This had been the first time this happened, and even though Kathy had trouble sleeping, she always made it a point to stay awake for the kids.

Standing up again, she held the cell phone in her hand in case Lonna would reply, and took a grip on Heather's arm lightly, starting to walk the girl toward the staircase.

"It's time for bed now guys, I'll go with you upstairs"   she said softly.   Her vision was clearer now, wearing her glasses again, and Kathy noticed Matthew still standing in the living room, faced away from them as he gazed through the dining room of the home.   He wasn't speaking, nor moving an inch as he stared ahead of himself, seeming lost in a deep thought in mind.   This made Kathy curious, and she tugged his arm for attention.   "C'mon Matty, I'm serious.   It's time for bed" she repeated.   The boy appeared deaf to Kathy's voice as his eyes viewed into the dark. He was looking across toward the back of the house, where the large window of the kitchen nook was in plain sight.   Matthew gave a tiny whisper from his lips without turning his head, and just enough for the girl beside him to catch a sense of fear in his voice.

"There's something…out there…"

Kathy again looked ahead, seeing the small reflection of the lamp in the living room to the side.   The window was like a painting.   A large glass-like painting, swallowing the wall it was placed in, and letting the inside world see out.   At first, there was nothing there.   The window just gave a ghostly black appeal while the hillside lingered behind it at the forest edge.   Moonlight of the sky gave the hill an eerie glow, just bright enough to see the 'something' Matthew spoke of. From what she could see, a figure was standing on the hill.   It wasn't visible at first, due to the dark surroundings, but it was there now.   Narrowing her eyes, Kathy tried to make out what it was, assuming firstly that a person was in the backyard.

Clutching the phone tightly, Heather held her arms around the babysitter's waist with a snug.   She too, could see it.   An eminent silhouette on the grass, neither solid, nor connective in appearance. The feeling it gave was unnerving as it looked back down at them.   It seemed to be watching silently, and not moving an inch of its façade.   She couldn't distinguish it.   There was no body, but merely a tall blackish blob.   A creature-like being, with no face or physical body revealed.

"What the hell…is that?…"   Kathy managed to say, staring out the window.   Matthew took in a deep breath of his own, while Heather started tugging repeatedly on Kathy's shirt.

"Kathyyy….I don't like iiiit…it scares me…" the young girl complained.   Kathy pulled on Matthew's arm again, trying to take him out of the unknown creature's view as she whispered.

"Matty…c'mon…stop looking at it"   she told him quietly, acting as though something may happen if they made any sudden movements.

What happened next, sent all three of them into a panicked state.   Seeing the figure on the hill had only been the beginning after Kathy made a move.   What was watching from afar, yet also rather near, finally made contact in the night. Almost in zigzagged pattern, the shadowed being fled down the hill in a rapid swoop, back and forth as it weaved across the lawn like a breeze.   In this moment Kathy's eyes grew large as whatever it was, suddenly crashed against the glass of the window, sending long fractured lines up the center.   The noise was fast, clear, and loud enough to make Heather scream when the bang erupted over the wall.   Like a split second, the figure was gone again as the cracked window remained...broken...but intact.   The shuttered noise made Matthew fall back into the girls behind him, letting Kathy fight for a balance on her own legs, attempting to catch her breath again.   It happened so fast, only the girl had time to scream, and only from the sound it made.   The babysitter knew now...*something*...was trying to get in at them.

Dialing quickly on her cell phone, Kathy flinched when Matthew stood up again, using her arm to help steady himself.   All three were shaken up by the attack, and Kathy was beginning to panic.   Her thoughts were erratic, not knowing who to call first; she dialed Lonna's number by second nature.   When the familiar voice of her friend came on the speaker, Kathy's words were rushed as they stood in the center of the room.

"Lonna!   Lonna I need you to come here right now!"   she demanded.   "There's something attacking us!"   Lonna moved her head away from the phone, giving the fact her friend was yelling in her ear.

"Whoa...slow down...what's attacking you?   What are you talking about?"   asked the other girl.   With their backs turned from the living room window, Kathy didn't notice the same figure rushing quickly toward them from behind in the same shifting manner.   It was swift, hitting the glass, and cracking it in several places as one side shattered along the exterior.   The larger windows of the home were double panned, and the second glass remained, only receiving major surface cracks.   This time Kathy screamed as well as Matthew and Heather, each of them backing away from the larger window and nearly falling to the floor again.   The being was nowhere in sight, as it seemed to only strike once and then leave. Lonna's face held a fix of shock and concern after hearing the sounds of the screams, and quickly jumped up from her bed.

"I-I'm on my way over, just hang on!"   she called back to them.   "Call the police!"

"Just hurry!   I don't know what it is!" Kathy replied.   Dropping the phone to the floor, Heather stepped on the screen, breaking the tiny glass into small pieces from the impact.   Kathy pushed the girl off, grabbing the small device as she tried to reconnect with Lonna again.   To no avail, the phone was now broken and the call was lost.   Heather apologized to the teen several times, starting to cry from the entire situation. Matthew took his sister in his arms again, leading her away from Kathy as the three of them ran into the small half-bathroom near the hallway.   The boy slammed the door shut, sitting on the floor with the others close to him.   The little room held only a toilet and sink, and no window for the 'attacker' to get at them, figuring this was a safer spot to hide.

Still in tears, Heather clung tightly to her brother's waist and stared at the door of the small room.   Kathy was sitting in front as the three of them huddled together now.   She motioned for the younger girl to stop crying, whispering that she wasn't angry with her breaking the phone, and held a finger to her lips.   As she began to quiet herself, Matthew looked up at Kathy again and tapped her shoulder.

"What are we supposed to do now?"   his whispered voiced questioned.   Kathy could tell the children were scared, and she knew their lives were in her protection.   She forced a smile over her trembling lips at the boy.

"We…wait here.   Before I lost the call, my friend said she would be here.   So we'll wait until she comes.   Just stay quiet for now"   she told him.   Heather laid her head upon Kathy's lap, falling out of Matthew's arms.   The boy leaned back against the wall beside the toilet, and Kathy peered out the crack between the doorframes.

"That thing is scary…it's a monster, Kathy….please don't let it get me…promise you won't let it…"   Heather mumbled lightly.   Softly stroking the girl's hair, the babysitter gently hushed the child in a calming tone to ease her mind.   The tiled floor of the room was cold, making the situation further uncomfortable and both girls shivered from it.   Matthew never spoke, leaning on the wall, he simply gazed around the small room he was in.   Lost in his own thoughts.   Possibly trying to calm himself in his own way, his fingernails scratching into his arm from a random itch.   He went over it several times until leaving his skin reddened from the scraping.   He acted as though he didn't even notice if he was causing any pain to himself.

"Matty stop it, you'll make it bleed"   Kathy warned.   She'd been staring over at him, wondering if he was alright.   Turning his eyes to her again, he stopped his hand, but remained silent.   Listening beyond the door, the teen heard nothing.   No sounds of breaking glass, nor even the ticking of the clock.   Though the room was dark, the light from the living room lamp gave a beam underneath the closed doorway, just enough for them to see the outlines of their bodies sitting together.   It was a terrible place to hide.   Chilling, diminutive, and awkward being surrounded by four walls seeming to close in around them.   Kathy wasn't afraid of closed spaces, but even *this* bathroom gave her claustrophobia.   Maybe it was just the situation.   After being attacked by something of unknown origin, and quickly retreating to a small hole-like spot in the dark wasn't the best option they could make.   Then again…what was?   The cell phone was damaged, and whatever was out there, had already broken two of the windows with ease.   Undoubtedly, this creature was strong enough to crack glass, let alone move with swift speed.   There was no telling what it would do if it actually came in contact with their bodies.   They hadn't even known whether or not it was human.   By now, Kathy discerned that it wasn't of this world, and though terrified, she was determined to keep the younger ones safe with her until Lonna arrived.   Part of her hoped the parents would come home soon, and cradle their children in their arms after she explained the situation.   However, she'd probably no longer be trusted enough for any future babysitting job, considering the Stafford's may not believe her.   Seeing the children frightened and Matty being injured slightly, along with the broken windows, Kathy realized she would have a lot on her hands now. This dilemma was going from bad to worse very quickly, and even if Lonna arrived to the house, by law, she wasn't allowed to take the kids away from the home without permission.   Granted, it was for their own safety, but giving the problem of not knowing what was attacking them, seeming non-human, there's a chance they wouldn't believe…unless seeing with their own eyes.

"You guys will have to help me explain this to your parents later.   There's a chance they won't believe me about this, and I could get into big trouble" Kathy whispered to them.   Both Matthew and Heather blinked their eyes, and then nodded slowly at the girl's words in agreement. Laying her head down on the teen's lap again, the younger girl closed her eyes as she rested and Kathy leaned against the wall, opposite of Matthew.

"Let's just…stay in here.   I don't really

wanna leave yet" Matthew said quietly. Kathy nodded to him, soon closing her own eyes as she held the child in her arms. Matthew folded his arms atop his knees, burying his face into them and staring down at the floor below. It was all silence now. Neither of them speaking, nor moving, but sitting in plain silence of darkness, not knowing what would happen next while waiting for Lonna to come to them.

Chapter 3

October 30th, 10:25pm

To remain motionless; a constant state of stillness in the darkness of a small room can make you feel numb. A dead-like feeling of not being able to move after sitting for a long period of time. Silence has a lengthy effect of teasing your brain into thinking you're deaf without the comfort of noise, if even just a slight tap could relish your ears again. It can make you feel insane, not knowing what you'll hear next after such elongated nothingness. No movement, no sound, and no life. Just quiet. The world in constant rest around you, letting you know you've been away for a very long time.

Kathy felt her own body jolt as she opened her eyes. Both Heather and Matthew lay sleeping on the floor in front of her as the pain from the kink in her neck shot into her back. She'd been leaning against the wall in this position for over an hour, and falling asleep for a short time until waking again. Although, it wasn't the silence that woke her. She'd gotten so used to it, that the slightest sound brought her conscious. She couldn't tell what it was, but something was in the hallway next to them. The living room lamp was still on, and still gleaming a gentle glow of yellow light under the door through the crack, except this time…something was blocking it half-way. A figure standing near the door…breathing a droning noise as the chilling breath floated through the cracks. She could feel it…waiting there. That thing again…was in the house…and watching them. Whatever it was, it knew they were there…but it wasn't moving. Just standing there and waiting. Waiting for them to move.

      Not knowing what to do, Kathy's heart began to race inside her chest. Her pupils dilated as she stared across the small room at the children and the wall, seeing it blur in pain from not blinking. She didn't want to blink…she was afraid to move. Afraid to move anything, even her eyelids. That creature was standing right beside her, and only separated with a plank of wood shaped into a closed door. It'd been thankfully locked, but she felt vulnerable. She felt the danger of the creature hindering over her body so near, and her eyes watering up from the burning pain. Finally blinking them as she could no longer endure. It was the only motion she could make without feeling she may lose herself. She'd stopped her own breathes, clutching her hands into balling fists, trying to contain her silence.   The children still slept there, and she hoped they wouldn't wake.

The figure's breathing was a hideous and morose sound...it crept into her body, alarming every organ and stirring through her veins as it touched her soul.   *'Go away...please...just...go away...'*   she thought to herself, too scared to move her lips and make a gasp.   Hearing the creature stroke the door, sliding something down the surface in a minor grazing sound.   It seemed to be testing it...feeling the texture of the wood between them and pressing against it.   She squeezed her fists tighter...her painted nails edging into the skin of her hands, and making them lightly bleed.   The new pain was barely noticed as she prayed inside her mind for the thing to disappear.   Hoping the kids would not wake up and cause alarm.   Praying for it to just leave them...alive.

Opening her eyes again in a sluggish manner, she realized something.   It was quiet again.   Just as before...the silence had come back. No longer was a figure standing by the door, but now the glowing light had returned, and the menacing sound of breaths were gone.   The coldness left her, and the children on the floor were waking up slowly to see her there.

"Kathy?   Are you okay?"   Heather

whispered, tapping the girl's arm for attention. Kathy had for most accounts been sitting there in a constant daze since opening her eyes again.   She relaxed her fists, now a reddish white color on her skin from the pressure, and the small trickles of blood from her piercing fingernails.   Matthew stared at the girl in concern and mouth lightly agape from her appearance.   She was breathing again, but only slightly as she came back to reality. Looking down at her hands, the boy quickly grabbed the toilet paper from the wall attachment beside him.   He began to wrap it around her hands to stop the bleeding, and she seemed to lay there motionless.   She let him wrap her wounds without speaking, only to look around the room as though inspecting its safety.   Leaning down to the floor, she peeked through the crack, seeing the objects of the living room just down the hallway. Matthew sat there, not knowing if he should continue, and let the paper roll fall to the floor.

"What happened to you?..."   he asked cautiously.   The teen turned her head to him, raising a finger to her lips, letting him know to keep quiet.   She didn't want to talk, for fear the figure may come back, and she was confused at how and why it suddenly left.   She prayed for it to leave...but she didn't think it actually would. Something wasn't right, and she knew this.   That creature was just too persistent to enter the home before, and it was probably just out there, waiting for them.   Waiting in the dark for them to leave the bathroom in an open area.   She figured it was easier for it to attack in larger space, since it hadn't entered the tiny room.

Breathing normally again, Kathy gave a sigh of relief and pulled the girl close in her arms. Heather was just too confused to ask, and willingly let the teen hold her again. In the distance, the sound of a car could be heard outside. Parking out front, near Kathy's Pontiac, and hearing the engine die off. Widening her eyes a bit, she realized this must be her friend. Lonna had finally arrived, and this made her heart skip another beat from relief and worry. Lonna lived at the other end of town, so it took her a while to arrive. Not knowing whether the figure had gone, she held the children back from the doorway as they all listened. The footsteps running up to the main entrance were fast, soon hearing a loud knocking on the door.

"That's your friend, Kathy. We should let her in" Heather said with a smile. The girl reached for the doorknob, only to be stopped by Kathy's hand in the way.

"No...not yet. Just...stay here" she demanded. Heather pulled herself from the teen's arms and sat on the floor by her brother with a look of annoyance. She was impatient and tired of sitting in the bathroom, and long since wanted to leave.

"I don't like it in here...I want to leave...I'm tired" the girl countered. Matthew also pulled his sister back from the door, feeling second nature of Kathy's request, noticing something must've happened when he was sleeping.

"If she wants us to stay, then we will. Be quiet" he said to her. Folding her arms and turning her head to the side, Heather felt disgusted and bored with the situation.

"You're only saying that 'cause ya like her" she retorted in sarcasm. Kathy shushed them both quickly as the front door opened, letting the guest enter the home. From what she could see, it was indeed Lonna, who was now standing in the living room and looking for them.

"You guys…I'm here…where are you?" she called out. Feeling safer now in the company of her friend, Kathy stood up and opened the door. Lonna walked down the hall to greet them, giving Kathy a light hug.

"Oh god, Lonna…I don't know what the hell it was, but I think it's still here somewhere…" Kathy said immediately. The look on her face easily shown her fear, and Lonna was worried.

"I came as soon as I could, but there was a lot of traffic on the way. Did you see who it was? Did you call the police yet?" she questioned. Ignoring her, Kathy looked around the room in several directions, making sure nothing else was out of the ordinary. She could still see the blood on the cracked kitchen window from the first attack, and after seeing the scrapes on the bathroom door, she felt uneasy again.

"Call the police, Lonna. Get them here

right away.   My phone is dead, and I think we're in danger here"   she said to her.   Seeing the seriousness in her friend's eyes, Lonna reached for her cell phone, and dialed for the police.   She'd never seen her friend so scared, and her voice was still shaken.   Sitting down on the couch again, Matthew held Heather close in his arms, making sure the girl wouldn't try to run anywhere as they waited.   Heather whined slightly, but after the babysitter's gesture to stop, she simply sat there quietly.   Lonna inspected the broken window in the living room, viewing the damage done by the unknown attacker.

"What did it look like?"   she asked again. Kathy shook her head, placing her hands over her eyes to rub and relieve them from the stress.

"I don't know….it wasn't…*human*"   she muttered.   Lonna stared for a moment, narrowing her eyes, thinking Kathy wasn't completely coherent.   She told the police on the phone about the situation, telling them of the broken windows and the children in need of their parents return.   After being reassured that they would be receiving help soon, she hung up the phone and stood beside her friend.

"Help is on the way, Kathy.   You just need to relax now…everything will be fine.   They told us to call their parents and just stay inside, keep the doors locked, and wait for them"   she explained.

With another shake of her head, and

turning away, Kathy felt stressed and concerned the creature may come back again.

"You don't understand, Lonna…you didn't *see* this thing…or *hear* it…like I did" her voice trembling in her lips as she began to cry. The warm tears sliding down her cheeks as she quickly wiped them away. Lonna pulled her close, hugging her arms around her to comfort her.

It was now, Matthew jumped up from the couch and pointed toward the kitchen window in alarm. His eyes were large in panic and his hand was shaking as his other arm wrapped itself around his sister hastily.

"It's there again!" he shouted, "It's by the window!"

Kathy quickly turned to see the shadowed figure at the window, staring in at them as the broken glass slowly fogged over from the heat of its concealed mouth. Lonna stood in shock, finally seeing what the others had been terrified of. It was close to them…just by the glass itself, and though Kathy pulled her friend's arm to keep her away, there was just no stopping it. The window shattered with immense force, seeing the blackened creature snake its way inside. Pinning her to the floor, Lonna screamed in terror for her friends to help her as the ghoulish beast pierced its mouth into the back of her neck. The fangs were large, white and sharp enough to puncture through the girl's neck completely, scraping against the floor below her body. They'd pierced through her, letting the river of blood flow out on the floor in front of Kathy and the children watching in horror.   Neither of them dared getting close to save her, and the screams in Lonna's throat merged into gulping cough sounds. She bit her own tongue from the pain of the attack, feeling her spine pulling out of her back as the creature dove into its meal.   Grabbing the boy and girl, Kathy led them from the room down the hall again as they ran in screams from the sight. It was real…all too real, and her friend was murdered right before her very eyes in a mess of gore.   She didn't want it to be real, but it *was*…and she was gone.   In a matter of seconds her friend was eaten alive by something she'd never seen before…or thought could exist.

   She saw the children running in front of her.   Matty and Heather, both so scared and nearly stumbling over their own feet as they ran toward the small bathroom again.   They were so young…not knowing what to do, or where to go. Their first initial instinct was just to get away, and find a safe place to hide from a monster that came into their haven.   They did not deserve this…she was meant to protect them, and now they were running for their lives.   She couldn't bear to think what would happen if it caught them.   The creature…wanting its fangs in their tender bodies, and make them its dessert.   It frightened her to think this…and shaking her mind out of the thought, Kathy soon found herself slamming into the open bathroom door.   The slender and solid object colliding with her forehead and face was enough to throw her backward, landing on the floor unconscious from the impact.   She was silent now.   Laying there motionless, seemingly in death.   No longer did she hear the sounds of the screaming children, nor the panic of her body running down the hall.   Merely cold and dark silence.   The quietness of her own mind was in her company, and she could feel it surrounding her.   It seemed to cradle her, telling her not to worry, yet knowing she must wake up again. Wake up and save the kids.   Keep them away and safe from the monster of the night.   Only she could do it, because it was her own responsibility. It was her job as a babysitter.   To watch and protect the children, until their parents came home again.   She was about to fail this mission, and lose to an attacking creature that stole her friend's life.   It angered her…as much as she was terrified of the siuation, it also angered her.   How dare it come and do this to them.   Take her friends away from her, and hunt them down like animals.   What right did this thing have…to just come in and kill them.   She would show it who was boss, for it was her duty.   Her promise to the parents on keeping them safe.   She would wake up from this unconscious state, and kill the very being that claimed the life of Lonna Wright.   She'd win this time, instead of running from her fears, and face the darkness in bravery.   Conquer it….and show the world who she really was inside.

Chapter 4

October 31st, 12:40am

Halloween

It was quiet here. The sounds had gone again when her eyes dimly opened to reveal a tiled ceiling above. This was new. It looked nothing like the same plastered wood ceiling of the Stafford home. This room was freezing inside…her breath was floating over her eyes as she stared above herself. What was this place? She knew immediately, it was not the house she collapsed in. There was no light. No windows, or doors, but simply a room. A vast empty room in the darkness as she lay there. Her head ached from the hardness of the metal table she was on, and as she tried to lean upward, she felt the restraints of buckled straps holding her down. She was lying on what appeared to be an operating table in the middle of a blank room, strapped down against her will. This is when she realized she was naked. Her bare skin shivering against the cold metal below her, and she immediately felt violated. There was no trace of anything in her memory about how she got here. Everything was new now, and completely different. As though she had teleported to a new place somehow, or was brought here against her will. No sign of Matty or Heather, or even the house itself. She was truly in a new place, and becoming scared very quickly.

Off to her right side, the sound of a locked door opened itself, showing a figure standing in the light of the entrance. She could tell it was a male, and seemed rather young, possibly a teenage male as he started wheeling a small cart into the room. The creaking metal wheels scraped on the linoleum floor as he stepped into the light. Although she tried to cover her nude self, feeling her privacy taken from her, the male stood over her laying body with a fixed grin in his thin lips. He gazed down at her without a word, keeping a sinister smile of wanting to toy with her. To Kathy's surprise, it was Matthew standing there, eyeing every inch of her body.

"Matty! What the fuck are you doing!" she yelled at him. Her voiced echoed loudly through the empty room, bouncing off the shadowed walls around the two. The boy said nothing to her. He simply gazed and kept his grin. Slowly moving a finger up to his lips, he motioned for Kathy not to speak, and then reached for the cart beside him.   His piercing eyes appeared silver in color while reflecting the light from the florescent bulb dangling from the ceiling. He never looked away as he lifted a large black disc off the table.   Kathy recognized it as a phonograph shellac.   More commonly known as a vinyl record.   Her brows lowered in confusion and she moved her head to the side as Matthew leaned close to her.   He whispered a haunting sound when he spoke.   It was crisp in the cold air and she could see his breath softly float through his teeth.

"Music..." he said to her with an echoed tone.   The disc had the words "Put On Your Old Grey Bonnet" by the Haydn Quartet written on the center label.   Kathy held her breath as he stared at her intently...*still* smiling widely and eerily inhuman-like.   She watched him turn away as he placed the record on an old gramophone beside them in the room.   Strangely, she hadn't remembered seeing it there before, but that was probably due to the darkness.   Placing the needle down on the groove, an aged melodic tune soon drifted out of the large speaker horn.   With the jerk of his body, Matthew grinned at Kathy continuously and slithered toward her again.   He stood above her body and trailed his eyes up and down her stark nudeness...giving the look of lewd satisfaction on his pale face.   He licked his lips while reaching toward the table with one hand. The girl sneered at him and watched his every

move, not knowing what he may do next.   On a small silver tray, laying and waiting for its purpose was an electronic operating circular saw.   It was small, but sharp enough to cut through bone, and surgeons often used them for heart transplant operations.

Kathy quickly shook her head back and forth, struggling to free herself from the restraints. The music was playing innocently, and oddly distracting in the background as she panicked. She had to get away from this...get away from this maddened child who was now ready to cut her open after flipping on the switch.   The sound of the saw was horrid as he leered down at her, grinning with his glowing white eyes...and wanting to penetrate her chest.   He looked as though he'd hack her body to pieces with no remorse, leaving the kind and gentle Matty she once knew behind.

"Oh god, Matty!   Don't do this!   Please stop!" she cried out to him,   "I'm your friend!"

He raised his arm high into the air...the shinning silver saw poised above her body as he readied himself to strike her.   She was dreaming...she *had* to be dreaming.   *'Please God...let me be dreaming!...'*   she told herself, over and over in her mind as his arm came down on her, letting a shattering scream escape her voice. It was so loud, she even scared herself, screaming out to the world for anyone to stop this boy from killing her.

She felt her cries...but felt no pain. In fact, there was nothing now. Not even any sound. Opening her eyes again, she could see that he was gone. Everything was gone again. The room, the table, the music, Matty and the operation saw had all vanished in the split second of her screaming voice. No longer was she strapped naked to a metal bed, but rather sitting on the floor of another room now, fully clothed and warm. Her hands were there in front of her, and so were her legs. Everything was okay now. She felt her body tingle and her heart racing, but...*she was okay*. There was no danger with her now...just quiet emptiness.

Attempting to stand again, Kathy fell slightly backward as she steadied her legs and weight. Breathing hard, she tried to calm her heart beats. They felt as though they were going to explode out of her chest. She was so confused by this. Was she really almost killed by him? What just happened to her? Why wasn't she at the house anymore? Even though she felt safe again, nothing was making sense. There were still no signs of life or anything familiar, and she hoped another experience like Matthew coming in to kill her wouldn't happen again.

Maybe she *really was* dreaming, and this was just her body's way of telling her she needed to wake up soon. She did, after all, have the problem of recurring nightmares, but she never felt anything like this before. The world around her was unpredictable, and held a feeling of risk. Something here was threatening her, and she needed to find out what it was.

Looking down on the spot where she'd been sitting, she could see the blankets of her own bed where she slept every night. Gasping lightly, she saw the walls of her bedroom around her, with the computer desk and dresser standing nearby. She was home again. She really had been dreaming all this time, and now just woke from it all. What a relief it was...to wake up in her own room again. The Stafford kids were probably just fine. She wasn't at their house after all, and Lonna was probably at home, sleeping soundly in bed next to her boyfriend.

Taking in a long and deep breath, Kathy smiled to herself, moving the covers off her body and she stood from the bed. She'd been asleep in her clothes again, which wasn't the first time, and she decided she would go see if her mother was awake. Sometimes she would be in the living room at night, having a small snack and watching late night TV programs to pass the time. Her mother was a lighter sleeper than her, and had been this way for years now. She knew, if anyone could comfort her after the nightmares, it would be her.

Walking up to her bedroom door, Kathy stopped herself at the sight of graying smoke drifting in from under the crack. The smell of something burning was filling her nose, and a flickering orange light was coming from the other side.   Her first thought, was that something was on fire in the house, and now she had to hurry and see what it was.   Grabbing the door handle, she opened it to find the hallway completely ablaze. Wall to wall, and floor to ceiling, were all in searing hot flames.   The fire charred and ate at the wood, engulfing it hungrily with a breeze as it moved toward her swiftly.   Kathy shrieked at the advancing inferno, slamming the door shut again before being burned alive.   Falling to the floor, and slamming her side on the floorboards, she covered her face in caution.

     This was crazed…it was one thing after the other.   Although, she was sure that this was real this time.   It had felt all too real to be a bad dream…and those flames had even singed her clothing from her near escape.   She was sweating profusely now, feeling the heat rising in the room from the fire on the other side.   She was trapped, and her only other escape would be the window. She would have to jump, undoubtedly putting her life further in danger, but it was better than burning alive in her own home.   In her mind, dying from a fall would be a more accepting fate if she were to truly die from this.

     Looking around her room after raising her head from the floor, Kathy saw how everything was now missing.   Her bed, dresser, and even her computer desk…all were gone.   No longer could she see the window leading out, and the doorway behind her was dark again. Her entire bedroom...now a vacant taciturn space with the walls to remain. Turning around again, she tried opening the door but to no avail. It would not budge, much less turn the knob. Here she was again...trapped in another place, where nothing was around her, and feeling alone. How many times would she have to endure this, was beyond her understanding. She wanted to know what was happening to her, and why. Maybe she really wasn't dreaming after all. If it felt this real...then it *was* real. No matter how unusual it seemed, this was real. She remembered when she was younger, how people told her to pinch herself, if she ever felt like she was sleeping and needed to wake up. It was a stupid thought...but even now she felt like trying it. Grabbing her own arm, she pinched the skin with her nails until the pain told her stop and give in. She let out a small yelp from injuring herself, and saw the small welt mark plain as black and white. She truly was awake...now she just needed to find out what was going on.

A distant faint sound caught her attention as she looked up ahead. In the same room...someone was with her. She was not as alone as she once thought, and this voice sounded familiar as well. It was a fragile crying; soft sobs coming from a girl in the corner where Kathy's bed used to be. She knew it was Heather's voice right away, but why she was crying was something she didn't understand. The small girl was knelt to the floor, faced away from her, moving her arm in slow motions in front of herself while she cried. Kathy wasn't sure, but from what she could hear, the girl seemed to be saying something.   Her mumbled words came out in quivered nature, carrying across the room.

"...they'll eat me...the dolls...they will eat me if I sleep...I can't sleep here...they will eat me...I must kill them...or the dolls will eat me here...must kill them..."

The phrase rolled out of her lips in constant repeat as Kathy approached her in the murkiness. Kneeling down behind the girl, Kathy could hear sounds of scissors snipping open and closed.   The blades leisurely coming together and opening again as they cut into something held within her hands.   The girl's arms were covered in blood, as well as her clothing.   Kathy was unable to see if it belonged to her or not.   Possibly,... from someone else.   The girl hadn't moved from the spot, preferring to sit there as she snipped the objects into several pieces.   Pokes and prods came from the snipping, and Kathy could feel the uneasiness in the air.   It was thick like a fog, and it felt constricting.   A choking feeling that wanted to surround her, preventing any move or escape.

"Heather..."   she spoke to the girl genially, "...what's wrong?..."

The younger girl stopped her movements, casually turning her eyes and head around to see Kathy knelt behind.   To Kathy's horrifying dismay...the girl's face was melting off her skull.

The skin...smoking from an unknown source of heat as it slid sluggishly off the bone to the floor in mushy piles. Each chunk making a wet slapping sound as they fell. Heather's eyes rolled back into their sockets, bleeding out and falling down inside their empty holes. Her mumbling ceased as she dropped a dismembered object to Kathy's knees. Lying in front of her, was clearly a baby doll...all ripped apart. It was cut and torn from the large shearing scissors held in Heather's right hand. She'd been cutting several dolls, now all lying piled on top of each other throughout the room. All of them...their hair cut off and eyes gouged out. Some of them rolling over the floor boards around Heather's feet. They rolled like marbles in aimless patterns, bumping into the severed limbs of plastic legs and arms lying about. The dolls were bleeding...every one of them...as though alive, yet still inanimate objects.

Kathy let out a gaping moan as the girl swung her arm, and stabbed the pointed scissors in her abdomen. The sharp silver blades pierced into her body easily, like cutting into butter. They wedged in through her liver and stomach lining. She gasped out tiny breathes, feeling the hot tears filling her eyes as her vision became a blur. The pain was so intense she could no longer sit up, and fell forward on the floor. Blacking out...the pain gradually stopped...and the aching subsided. She felt dead. She *must* be dead. She couldn't feel anything now. There was nothing. No vision or sound. No feeling or sensibility.   No breathing.   She was dead now…and sure of it.   Going to another place in time…maybe Heaven…or Hell…whatever it may be.   She was gone now.

Chapter 5

November 6th, 8:30am

Sitting up quickly in her bed, Kathy glanced around her room as she held her hands over her stomach. She woke in a screaming daze, drawing the attention of the morning nursing staff in the hallway outside of her room. Opening her door, a tall Black-American woman came in and sat herself down on the bed, speaking with a calming voice. Her tone was slightly deep, but very genial and it focused the girl's attention.

"Are you alright Miss Bell?" she asked her, lightly taking hold of Kathy's arm and calculating a pulse. "Was it another nightmare?"

Feeling dumbfounded, the girl remained sitting in the hospital bed, looking around the small room she'd been sleeping in. This woman was unfamiliar at first...but only at first. Kathy would soon recognize her as Dr. Sandra Whitmore, one of the lead psychiatrists assigned to her case file. She would soon remember everything now...regaining a steady breathing habit again after a long night of deranged night terrors.

"Today is a visitation day. Would you like me to call your mother, and see if she can stop by?" the woman questioned. Kathy, still remaining quiet, nodded to the doctor and made a smile as she brushed the long bangs of her dark hair from her eyes.

She was in reality now...and even though she hadn't spoken to the woman, she pulled the covers up close to her body again. The doctor handed the girl a small red book, which Kathy had been using to keep a "diary of dreams" since the time of her first night in the building. It'd been a plan that she and the doctor made together, to document the occurrences that went on within her nightmares during the night. Every morning before breakfast, she would make another entry and start a new day of therapy within the hospital. It was the recent nightmare that made Kathy suddenly go through the night before Halloween again in her mind. She'd been a guest at the hospital's psychology ward for a week now, and was making little progress every day. Dr. Whitmore was planning to discharge her back home this very day, even with Kathy's recent episode. It was concluded, that the girl's psyche would experience these kinds of nightmares possibly for the rest of her life, and medication would be considered for a helpful solution.

Across the other end of town, the father of the Stafford family casually raked the autumn leaves on his back lawn to the piles by his driveway.   His children, Matthew and Heather were gone at school, and his wife was busy indoors with the daily chores.   It was a steady breezy morning, and even though it was late in the year already, he felt warm.   Setting his rake aside and deciding to take a break, he began to walk back toward the house again from the rear. Catching a glimpse of his eye, he stopped for a moment by the kitchen nook window facing the forest hill behind his home.   There, lying on the ground below the window was a squirrel.   He narrowed his eyes and cringed a bit from the dead animal's condition, seeing two large holes pierced into its flesh on the side.   It looked as though it'd been drained upon death, and left to lie on his lawn as a gift.   Something that cats often do for their owners, except…they don't typically drain the blood from animals.   The squirrel's skin had sagged tightly around the bones of the carcass. Ironically, the only seeming bite marks were just the two puncture holes in the side.   Indicating whatever had killed it….used a pair of long frontal fangs.   The sight of this dead creature made Edward Stafford feel uneasy.   He wasted no time in placing the corpse inside his trash bin.   The wind was sinking grimly around him now, and the warmth he once felt quickly dissipated.   What is it about a dead body, no matter human or animal...that makes us feel vulnerable inside? Maybe it's the fact we've come face to face with a lifeless being no longer capable of moving in our constantly changing world.   It makes us feel odd to see something so out of place in our existence. It stops us in our tracks, and we question our deepest thoughts.   The forest gave a creeping vibe as it loomed behind the man.   The breeze captured every sound, from the rustling of leaves, to the crackling of branches.   He stared into the trees for several minutes before moving again. Just barely...sliding softly through the thicket...his eyes caught a shifting shadow in the shades.   The kind of shadow that disappears after you've blinked.   The voice of Mrs. Stafford jogged Edward's mind out of his gaze, and he turned back toward the home.   So easily we disregard what is truly lurking around us...and every so often...very closely nearby.

"It wasn't a dream, you know..."   the low voice crept through Kathy's ears as her eyes opened gently.   She focused on the wall ahead of her as a figure slowly came into view beside her. Standing in the doorway was a man in formal black suit and tie.   He was steadfast with his hands held together in front of himself as he stared at her intently.   His hair, dark as his suit, was combed and cropped formally as well.   Most of it was hidden underneath a black fedora hat.   His face was very pale and featureless while his eyes were hidden tightly behind large round sunglasses.   The lenses were retro styled, and possibly from the 1960s decade.   They gave the alien-like impression of large black pupils gazing widely in her direction.   She hadn't noticed him there before while relaxing in the hospital bed.   She didn't even know how long he'd been there while her eyes were closed.   Furthermore...*when*...had she closed her eyes.   Kathy suddenly couldn't remember.

"...You weren't dreaming then...and you're not dreaming now"   he continued.   His voice was young, slow, and somewhat giddy in tone.   He didn't seem excited, but he sounded rather odd for his appearance.   It almost didn't match his body.   Much lighter and robotic than what she expected it to be.   Everyone suspects how a person's voice sounds when first meeting someone they don't know, and very few are ever surprised when they first hear it.

"What do you mean?"   Kathy replied delicately.   This was her first time speaking since waking up, and her mouth was a bit dry.   The man moved one of his arms behind him without diverting his gaze away from the girl, and shut the door of the room calmly.   He did this in such a way that one would surely have to practice several times to get it right.   It just didn't look natural.

"Well...most of it *wasn't* a dream...but some of it *was*"   he answered, cocking his head slyly to one side like a curious cat.   Kathy's brows narrowed above her eyes, and sat up in the bed quickly.

"Who are you?" she asked him, louder than before and swallowing to wet her throat. The man stepped forward twice and stopped by her bed, leaning forward enough to make Kathy want to move back in the awkward situation.

"Young woman,...you may call me Mr. White. I work for a highly organized, yet highly *secret* government group, under strict orders *not* to tell you who they are, or what they do" he said specifically and clear. "I am here because you have been in contact with a rather...*extraordinary* being. One that is *not* of this world" he clarified. Kathy gazed at her reflection in the man's dark sunglasses as he loomed above her. His breath was scentless, and she felt an unusual waft of heat coming from his body. His face was so perfect...almost too perfect. Not one scratch, mark or mole to be found. Not even hairline from where he could've shaved the day before like most men would have. Of course, it was possible he was wearing make-up. Not very common for men, but still very possible. She finally realized what his voice reminded her of, and that was the old radio personalities of the 1940s and 50s. Mr. White literally sounded like he was going to announce the next commercial for a new family car, or the latest brand of cigarettes. Except, he wasn't excited. He was giddy...but not excited.

"You're starting to creep me out" Kathy breathed, nearly disregarding what the man just said.   Mr. White quickly bent his body back upward again and stepped back.

"My apologies, Miss Bell.   I was merely trying to inform you of your situation"   he explained without a change of tone.   Brushing her hair to the side, Kathy looked up at him again.

"And what situation is that?"   she asked. She was both curious and nervous of this man's sudden emergence in her room, but it was hard to ignore his presence.   As though simply ignoring him was the wrong thing to do.   He gave off the impression of someone very important and powerful, and listening to what he had to say would be wise.

"The situation that has brought me here today"   Mr. White explained.   "Miss Bell…you, along with two other children, were recently attacked by something you could not indentify…am I *correct*?"   he questioned. Kathy's eyes widened a bit, and her head slowly nodded.   Why she didn't speak was a question even to herself.

"And this being…this *creature* of the shadows…proceeded to *devour* your friend, Lonna in front of your eyes…*correct*?"   he asked again. Kathy could feel the tears forming in her eyes now as she continued to nod.   Her emotions were welling up inside with the man's questions, and he forced her to recall the events of the night before Halloween in the Stafford home.   It was an overwhelming and confusing feeling.   She didn't know what to say next, and it seemed this man already knew what had happened without even being there.

"Miss Bell...the creature you encountered that night...is one that I have been seeking for a while now.   I have been hunting it for years...just as others like it in the past"   Mr. White continued. "You see,...this...*specter* of the dark that came to feast upon you and the children...is a vicious species of no name.   One of mysterious origins, from a world beside our own.   They come here for human nourishment, stalking prey within the shadows and disguising their forms.   I assure you...they are *very* clever about doing this...and have been killing humans and animals for centuries"   the man warned.   Kathy's eyes were wide with attention and her lip was softly quivering.   She wiped the tears from her face and held her arms against her chest.   She felt cold and violated, and the room was beginning to spin around her.   She soon felt Mr. White's unusually warm hands touch her face, and he laid her body back against the pillow.   It was strange how comfortable she felt when he touched her.   She somehow knew he wasn't going to cause any physical harm.

"Why did it attack us?   The creature from the forest...why did it come to *us?*"   Kathy asked him.   Mr. White stood up calmly again, and stared at the girl nearly a minute before replying.   As though debating with himself on whether or not he would continue divulging information.

"It wanted *you* most of all, Kathleen.   The

nightmares you've been having all these years, are manifestations of the creature toying with your mind.   It has been stalking you this way, because it is still young in age.   It has been growing for nearly as long as you have been.   In fact, the being arrived to our world just a day before your birth. More than likely attracted to your tender soul and energy, and residing in your mind for several years until it became strong enough to form a body of its own.   They first come to our world in tiny pods no larger than a piece of corn, and must act as a parasite and grow within a host for a short period. In time, they eventually eat their host and continue on to find other sources of food.   They do this by taking on various forms to lure victims.   They are shape-shifters by nature, capable of looking like any*one* or any*thing.*

The one stalking *you* was simply not strong enough to do this yet, and acted rather...*immaturely*...and...*impatiently*...trying to encompass you once again.   It was a foolish endeavor for its kind, and other members of its species would be very ashamed of its actions for not being more...*discreet*...while hunting"   Mr. White declared.   He slowly raised a hand up to his sunglasses to stop them from slipping down his perfectly pale face.   He was careful not to reveal himself any further than what he already had. Kathy, leaning forward again after steadying herself from the dizziness, began to shake her head slightly after hearing the man's words.

"But...how do you know it was attacking me

and the Stafford kids? How was...this creature...able to leave my body without me knowing?" she asked quickly, becoming more serious now. Mr. White narrowed his eyes at the girl's sudden displeasure. She couldn't see them behind the sunglasses, but from the movement of his face, she could tell he was narrowing them and feeling annoyed with her.

"I already told you...it was still *inexperienced* and *impatient.* It most likely left your body one night in your sleep. Thinking it was *mature* enough to live on its own...only to realize it craved the taste of your flesh the more it was away from you. I have met others of its kind in past. *One* in particular...was very strong indeed. It was able to create an entire warp through the dimension it came from...entrapping a young woman in a snare that nearly killed her. She was lucky to escape its wrath. At the time, it was the strongest I had ever come to face" Mr. White explained carefully. "*Yours*...is very much obsessed with you."

Taking in a deep breath, Kathy placed her head in her hands for a moment to think and take in everything the man had told her. It was truly a fantastical situation to believe...and yet it strangely began to make sense to her. Disregarding the fact he was someone she'd never met before, and had knowledge of something she couldn't understand completely, it still seemed to be very plausible in her mind. Most people wouldn't believe him right away, but after so many years of doctors and her parents not believing everything she experienced in her nightmares; Kathy was willing to trust this man now. He obviously knew things about her situation without her even having to tell him, and she'd never met him before until today. She had seen the entity in her dreams before. It was the one thing about the creature that seemed familiar to her on the night of the attacks. It still didn't change the fact she now felt very much in danger of being attacked again, no matter where she went.

"If...this *thing* is obsessed with me like you say...what am I supposed to do about it?" she asked him. "How do I keep myself safe from it?" Mr. White raised a brow behind his sunglasses and held his hands together in front of himself like before. Content in his position of authority.

"You *don't.* You would have to be sure to *never* go back to the Stafford home again, since it found you there. These creatures have long memories, Miss Bell. Once they fixate on you...they rarely *ever* stop hunting" the man explained dryly. His tone was very matter-of-fact and cold. He seemed unsympathetic and sarcastic about the entire matter at hand.

"So then...there's no hope for me" Kathy said, staring down at her blanket. "You're telling me...some unexplainable creature...is going to try and kill me again, and I have no way to stop it? Well fuck you then. I don't need to believe this shit anymore" she replied angrily. Mr. White stood emotionless at the girl's remark, and tilted his head to the side again very slowly.   A loud crack shifted beneath his skin and Kathy's eyes squinted from the sound.   If he was angry with the girl, then he could hold his anger well.   He probably came here knowing she would have some hostility toward him anyway, and he prepared for it.

"*However...*"   he began to say, and Kathy glared at him from the bed,   "...the creature is aware of my presence...and will surely not try another attack as long as I am here in this town" he assured.   Kathy gave a short huff-like laugh at the man's words without smiling.   It made sense, though.   During her stay at the hospital for a week, obviously nothing of the sort had come to attack her again.   Maybe this man was telling the truth after all.

"So then what am I to do?"   she asked him.

"You are being discharged from this hospital, Miss Bell.   Your mother is on her way here even as I speak.   You are to go home...and *stay* there for as long as I'm in town.   I will come to your residence after I've destroyed the beast and fulfilled my duty"   Mr. White clarified. Kathy raised her brows and swallowed hard.

"Your *duty?*   You mean...you're here to *kill* it?   Just *you?*"   she questioned him.   Mr. White did his favorite little cock of the head, and answered her quickly.

"*Yes*...Miss Bell.   Just me.   It is my job here, and you are *not* to interfere or warn others of the creature's presence.   We don't need a panic in this town.   Do you understand?"   he warned, raising the seriousness of his tone.   Kathy shifted her eyes, but nodded to the man.

"I understand"   she said softly.   Mr. White slowly tipped his hat to the young woman, and turned away toward the door.

"Then I shall leave.   We will meet again very soon, Miss Bell"   he announced.

"Wait!"   Kathy called out to him, as the man turned to face her.   "Is…Lonna…?"

"Yes, Miss Bell.   Lonna Wright is dead.   Her death occurred the night you entered a separate dimension created by the creature to lure you.   Lonna unknowingly entered the same trap, and fell victim to the being's hunger.   It then proceeded to try and locate you within the home, but was interrupted when the children's parents arrived on the scene.   *You* had fallen unconscious, and were brought here for medical attention.   Upon your departure, the creature's separate reality had lifted and the children have no memory of what happened that night.   Nor is the Stafford home still damaged from the creature's attacks.   It is as if nothing had ever happened at all.   No one but you and I will know of Lonna's death, because it happened in another world.   Her sudden disappearance has been ruled out as a missing person's case, since her body is nowhere to be found.   In time, her parents will accept her fate as an unsolved mystery.   A possible runaway.   As you see…this creature must be stopped. "   he said precisely.   Without further conversation, he left the room and closed the door behind him.

Chapter 6

The air was chilled on Kathy's face as she and her mother exited the hospital toward the parking lot.   The kind of chilled air that annoyingly gripped every nerve down to your bone after a heavy rainstorm has fallen.   She could still feel the dampness, and smell the worms in the grass while tiny droplets of the rain continued to trickle.   The storm had passed, but the clouds still lingered.   It was twilight now, getting closer to evening and the sun was setting quickly.   Her mother held her daughter's hand comfortingly, and was in no hurry to the car.   The white Chrysler LeBaron convertible with a black top was just ahead of them, sitting neatly among the rows of cars.   Kathy noticed it was parked on the end, as her mother always seemed to do this. She once mentioned how she disliked parking in between vehicles, for fear of people slamming their car doors into her own car.   As it happened once in the past.   There was still a long scratch in the paint on the passenger side from the previous incident.

"Are you happy to be coming home again?" her mother asked her, breaking a silence between them.   "You haven't said a word since we left the building."

This was true of course, in both ways.   Kathy seemed to be in a trance state, and only cared to stare ahead of herself in thought.   She knew her mother was only concerned, but she didn't know if she should mention any details about the mysterious Mr. White and the warning he gave her.   She suddenly wanted to tell her everything he said, but she also feared that her mother may not believe her.

"I'm fine, Mom.   Just tired really"   she replied quietly.   They approached the car, and her mother immediately unlocked it.

"We'll be home soon enough, dear.   I'm making spaghetti tonight.   I know it's your favorite" she announced. This little bit of news actually brought a smile to Kathy's face, if even for a moment. She was indeed very hungry, and felt like she hadn't had a proper meal in ages.

"That sounds great actually" she said, sliding herself into the car. Her mother simply smiled in response, and started the engine. The top of the convertible was up and locked tightly, and Kathy was glad for this. It was just too cold out for it to be down. Her mother had a habit of putting it down too often, even if the weather wasn't permitting. The only thing that seemed to stop her from doing so was rain and snow.

The trees became a blur with the fading orange glow of sunlight quickly disappearing. Kathy remembered being very young and wondering if the sun was actually dying every night, and being reborn again every morning. She recalled how she hated the night, and the moon was too mysterious in the darkness. She always wanted the light to come back…but now…it was different. The night was intriguing, and a mystery all its own. There were wonders in the night that many were too careless to notice…and therefore, would never know about. The moonrise was pale and bright when it pierced through the black clouds, illuminating the sky in a show of magical whitish blue hues.   Aligning the clouds, and shimmering off the frozen ice miles above the planet's surface.   The moon was romancing the dark, and Kathy was falling in love with it.   Her mother turned on the radio for noise and the static rose in the silence.   Kathy continued to stare into the night while her mother fiddled with stereo knobs, turning them back and forth until a low melody drifted out of the speakers.   Kathy's eyes diverted toward the radio suddenly and she held her breath.   The song was the same one from her dream…the one that little Matty played on the gramophone just before he tried to kill her.   The chorus of "Put On Your Old Grey Bonnet" cheerfully greeted her with crackles of static between the words.   She remembered Matty's devilish grin, and the mouth full of shiny teeth that gleamed at her with his narrow glowing eyes.   It made her skin crawl again just thinking of it.   The way his dead-cold fingertips had touched her naked body on the metal bed gave Kathy a harsh chill.   It was as though it really happened, even though Mr. White said it was all in her mind…from the creature.   The thing that tried to *eat* her.

Mrs. Bell rolled her eyes and stopped playing with the radio to focus on the road. The song continued to play, somewhat eerily through the static, which only made it sound older than what it was.

"It's better than the silence, I guess" her mother said finally. Kathy immediately reached over and switched it off, gaining a look of displeasure from the mother just then. The car came to a slow halt in the middle of the empty street, and the woman faced her daughter.

"What the hell is going on, Kathy? Why are you acting so distant all of a sudden?" she questioned her. Kathy was visibly shaking and her mother took hold of her arm to steady her.

"I...don't...feel well" she muttered, falling forward in her own hands. She held her head in a dizzying daze, trying to stop the world from spinning in her vision. Mrs. Bell looked back at the road to pull the car over to the curb, and noticed something standing in the street. It was a tall black figure with a narrow feature and a faceless head peering down the roadway at them. It stood motionless in a misting fog enveloping the area around its body. It appeared to have no legs...nor a physical shape to help the woman comprehend what it truly was.   She wasn't sure if it was standing or floating in the wind.   It looked like a cloaked man standing in the darkness, but the air never moved any fabric that would come from his dark clothing.   The woman's mind began to ponder as to what it could be…whether a blackish silky skin…made of a goo substance, or a heavy piece of clothing unable to move.   It seemed to be both at once, and this scene made the woman touch her daughter's shoulder for attention.

"What is…*that*…?"   she whispered.   Kathy slowly raised her eyes to meet the road above the dashboard.   Her vision faded together again and she gasped loudly.   The unusually shaped being then jerked its head backward as a long and deep shrill loudly cried out through the air.   It made the women cover their ears in fright, and they watched in horror at the cadaverous creature jolt itself high above the road into the sky.   The trees along the street shook immensely in the sound, and the car's windshield cracked a snake-like fissure from right to left.   This made them scream inside the vehicle, and the static-filled radio signal silenced instantly.   Uncovering their ears, the woman listened for any amount of sound in the night…but there wasn't any.   Kathy watched her mother speak, but no words could be heard from her lips.   It was the same for Mrs. Bell when Kathy shouted her name.   She shouted as loud as she could…but the world was muted around them. Not even the car's engine made a noise while continuing to run languidly.   It was loud silence. The kind of taciturnity that made you feel like you're deaf.   So quiet…you could go insane from lack of sound.   An aching feeling deep within your brain that made you panic and search frantically for any mode of noise.   *Anything…*to make a sound.

The radio needle shifted to one side and stopped there.   The speakers gently dribbling out a voice in the hollowness of the void they sat within.   It crackled rough and far into their ears…a slithering sharp whisper vibrating the windows beside them.

"….Kaaaaathyyyyy…

…IIIIII…waaaaannnnt…youuuuu…"

The girl covered her ears again in tears while her mother screamed uncontrollably.   The sound exploded all around the heads as the creature tore off the convertible's top with immense force. Sending jagged lines through the broken glass of the windshield when it shattered.   The pieces flew through the air as the car leapt upward from the grip of the monster looming above them.

Kathy's mother stomped on the vehicle's gas pedal and the car bolted forward in the dark.   The speedometer needle reached seventy by the end of the street and the chilling wind blew wildly around their faces.   Mrs. Bell turned the wheel abruptly, seeing a row of parked cars at the road's end, and the convertible slid down the wet asphalt out of control.   It smashed into a parked station wagon with a thunderous collision of glass and scrapping metal.   The car buckled itself into the wagon's side so hard and loud, that Mrs. Bell's forehead slammed against the steering wheel. Her head fell to one side with no sense of direction.   The car had struck the wagon on its left side, with Kathy facing the street they just came from.   The horn blared for a few moments, until dying off from the damaged wires.   Kathy's eyes drearily stared at the sky as she lay in the car without moving.   Her leg was twisted and broken under the dashboard, strangely not giving any pain…or she was simply paralyzed.   She could tell from the cold that was surrounding her tender body now.   A streetlamp casually fell on its side, with the bulb shattering on the road aimlessly. It'd been dismembered from its bolts during the impact of the crash.   The sound of the breaking bulb was almost delicate compared to the roaring smash that Kathy just witnessed.   At this moment she could feel her eyes closing softly from exhaustion and her arms didn't care to move. The pain was coming now…tiny jolts at first, followed by a steady ache of raging throbs deep around her severed bones.   She clutched her leg in tears and wordless moans as he eyes opened again.   She found the shapeless creature standing over her behind the car.   Her breath sunk in her throat as she watched its razor sharp fangs slide through the mushiness of its eyeless face.   A large hole opened wide around its body as the teeth multiplied in countless numbers.   No eyes glared at her…just rows upon rows of elongating white teeth ready to sheer her body to pieces.   Her scream was met with a loud electrifying gunshot in the night air, and the creature's body shrieked from the wound through its gooey structure.   A bright show of electricity bolted through the monster in sparks and fire until the creature could no longer stand the pain.   The remains made a burst as the silky substance spewed across the cars and the covered the ground in messy black slime.   The glop covered Kathy's body, and was hot to the touch.   It nearly felt like it was burning her skin, and she frantically wiped it off.   She gasped for fresh air, and fell out of the car when the door broke loose.   Lifting her head, she saw a shiny pair of black shoes standing ahead of her in the slime.   They stepped closer and she felt her body being lifted carefully off the ground, and stood up again.   Kathy's tired eyes met with a pair of dark sunglasses covering the eyes of a man with a familiar pale face.

"Looks like I got here just in time, Miss Bell" the man said, speaking his familiar giddy tone of voice.   Kathy realized now it was Mr. White, and he was helping her to regain her stance.   She immediately began to cry and buried her face into his unusually warm body.   The man seemed puzzled by this reaction, but he knew why she did it.   He somewhat reluctantly, placed his own arms around the girl to comfort her.   "There, there now…it's all over.   The creature won't be coming back"   he reassured.   Kathy raised her head and wiped her tears to look upon her savior with a thankful smile.   She never thought she'd be so glad to see this strange man ever again, but he was all she could've hoped for in this moment. Standing behind Mr. White, the girl noticed several men dressed in similar black suits…all wearing the same dark sunglasses over their pale faces.   They were sporting the same retro hairstyle, under their black fedora hats.   They spoke no words as Mr. White motioned them toward the scene.   The men immediately attended to the wreckage and Kathy's mother lying in the car.

"Will she be okay?" Kathy asked the man, her voice sounding very small and child-like. She was innocent and helpless in the arms of someone she barely knew. Mr. White gave a quick nod, and raised a large silver weapon in his hand. It was a very unusual looking gun...seeming to be made entirely of a chrome-like substance, or another silvery metal of sorts. Clearly unidentifiable and probably only used by the government. It was longer than Kathy's entire head, and its appearance made her deduce it was the cause of the creature's demise.

"Your mother will live. She is merely wounded and unconscious from this *terrible* ordeal. This area is being quarantined, and you and your mother will be coming with us for an undetermined amount of days until we feel you are both *cleansed* completely" Mr. White explained. Kathy noticed her mother's eyes opening slowly, and being carried away to a large black van by several of the men in suits. She released the man from her hold, and swallowed before speaking again.

"Are there...more of them?" she asked quietly. Her eyes were gleaming curiously into the man's dark lenses. Mr. White gave a light sigh and looked around the street, as though he was surveying the scene before he would reply.

"Yes, Miss Bell.   There are more of these beings.   That is why I keep them *out* of this world. I keep them where they belong.   *Away*...from humans.   They are alien demons of the very sort, and have occasionally breached the human world for many years.   They will surely do it again...and then I will destroy one again"   he declared. Kathy held her arms across her stomach gently, listening with intent at the man's words.   He was genuine and truthful.   She could tell he had no reason to lie about this.   Not after everything she'd seen with her own eyes.

"You know a lot about them...don't you?" she asked.   Mr. White cocked his head like a cat again, and nodded.

"Yes I do"   he answered specifically. Kathy made a slight smile and nodded to him again.   She placed her hands casually on her hips, and narrowed her eyes.

"Are *you* an alien too?"   she asked again, getting straight to the point of her curiosity.   Mr. White slowly folded his arms together in a dominant pose, with his large silvery weapon poking high above his shoulder.

"I am no more alien...*nor human*...than any of us truly are in the vast universe that surrounds us, Miss Bell..." he said with a careful tone. He lifted sunglasses off his face gently, revealing his eyes glowing gently in the darkness of the night. They shone wide in shape, angular and black...but a lighter shade of black...with silvery gray pupils in the centers. Kathy formed a small smile...and nodded very slowly to the unusual man standing before her. "...and I will leave you with those thoughts."

Conclusion

     My name is Kathleen Bell.   Ever since I was a young girl, I've suffered from frequent nightmares.   Granted, as I grew older they've seemed to dissipate, but they still return to this day.   These were not your regular nightmares.   I was once told they could've been "night terrors" which are common among young children.   These dreams would haunt me on a nightly basis, waking me to the point of screaming out through sleep.   I would see things you couldn't even imagine, and still haven't forgotten.

     By the age of eighteen, I was diagnosed with what is known as "Pavor Nocturnus" and placed in a psychiatric hospital for recurring Psychotherapy.   This diagnosis is very real, and can be found in patients from all over the world to this day.   Also known as night terrors, this sleep disorder involves abrupt awakening from sleep in a terrified state.   It occurs approximately 90 minutes after sleep during stage 3 or 4 NREM sleep.   Often known as a parasomnia disorder, characterized by extreme terror and a temporary inability to regain full consciousness.

I now know *who* and *what* was causing it.

You know my name is Kathleen....but to Mr. White, and to *other* beings...

...I am also known as Agent Bell.

The nightmares haven't stopped...I just have new ones now...

...and my life will never be the same.

From the Author

The entirety of this short story is a work of fiction, although the diagnoses of Pavor Nocturnus, and the inspiration for this story are both real.   Years ago, on Halloween night when I was thirteen, my aunt came over to baby-sit me and one of my younger sisters.   We had just got back from candy collecting, and my parents at the time, had gone out to buy some soda and ice cream for a movie night.   During this time, I lived in a house very similar to the one I described in this story, all down to detail.   Except it was in another Pennsylvania town, and not in Oil City.   Even the large windows from the kitchen and living room areas were real.   If one would stand at either end of the house during the day, they could easily peer through it to the other side if the curtains were open.   On this night, my aunt and I noticed someone, or something standing on the back lawn at the edge of the hill in front of the trees.   She and I made the thought of it looking like some kind of ghostly figure staring down at us in the night. It never moved from that spot, not even after the family came back home again, and the next morning it was nowhere to be found.

To this very day, I have no idea who or what it was, and the dead squirrel in the story, was actually two dead birds found on the lawn in the span of the next two following days. November 1st and 2nd. Later on, I reproached my aunt on this subject, and after having denied it, I still wonder if she truly thinks about it or remembers. I still remember the terrified look on her face when we couldn't exactly figure out what it was, and also to this day, my sister doesn't seem to remember it either. I don't really scare easy from paranormal phenomena, if that's truly what it was, so this is more of an interesting memory to me, rather than something to forget. Granted, it spooked me that night, as it probably would have any child. I've always loved to read and write, and my creative mind is always active. I personally love the paranormal - for its one subject we don't know everything about, and can have different results every time we study it. Our world is truly a living wonder of mysteries. You never know what exactly is really out there on your backyards, watching with those silent eyes…and the day and night respectfully hold their different secrets.

Printed in Poland
by Amazon Fulfillment
Poland Sp. z o.o., Wrocław